This book is for Maria Dalton, Eliza Carthy,
and Jackie Morris, with love and admiration
V.F.

To Derek Cobley, who, through
the Swansea Wordplay festival,
reached out into the imagination
of so many children
J.M.

EGMONT
We bring stories to life

First published in Great Britain in 2001
by Walker Books Limited in *Singing to the Sun and Other Magical Tales*
Published in this edition by arrangement with Walker Books Limited, London.
This edition published 2008
by Egmont UK Limited,
239 Kensington High Street,
London W8 6SA

Text copyright © Vivian French 2001
Illustrations copyright © Jackie Morris 2008
The author and illustrator have asserted their moral rights
A CIP catalogue record for this title is available from The British Library

ISBN 978 1 4052 2751 3

1 3 5 7 9 10 8 6 4 2

Printed in Italy
Colour Reproduction by Dot Gradations Ltd, UK

www.egmont.co.uk
www.jackiemorris.co.uk

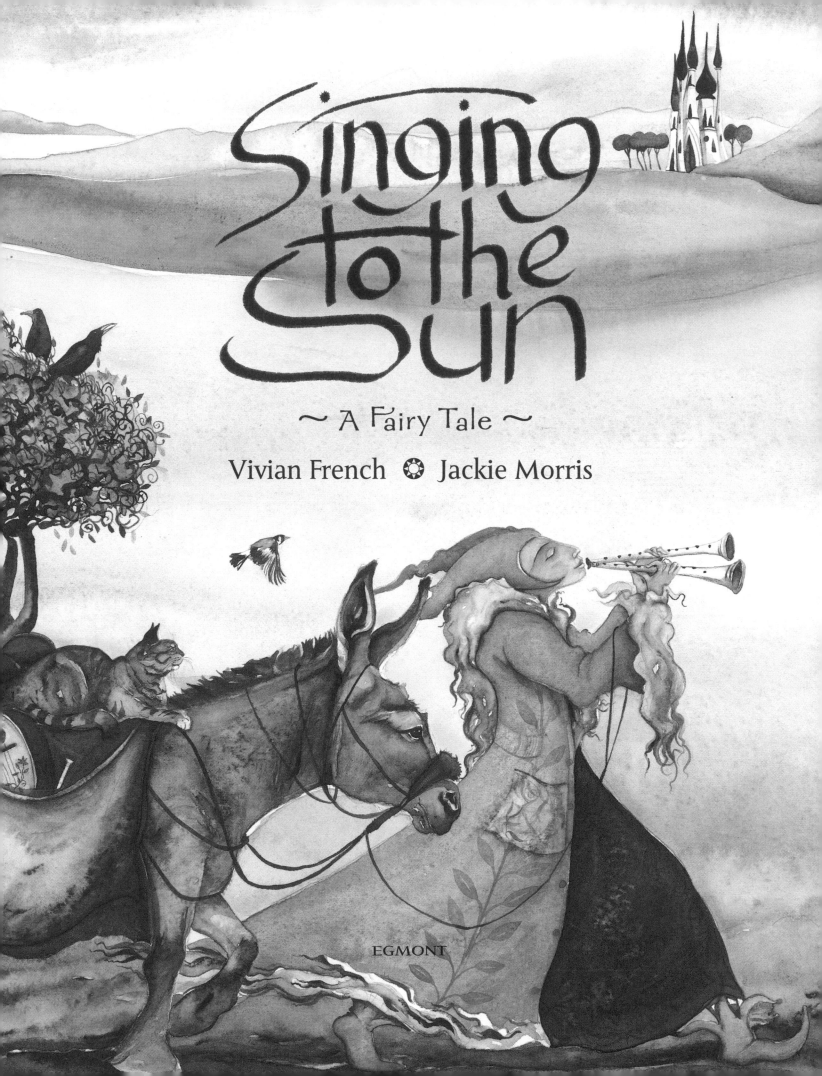

Singing to the Sun

~ A Fairy Tale ~

Vivian French ✷ Jackie Morris

EGMONT

Once there was a lord who did not believe in love.

He married a lady who believed only in gold, and at the end of a year they had a son.

"One day," said the lord, "this child will be the most powerful man in all the land. Even the mightiest of my horses will bow as he walks by."

The small tabby cat who sat by the hearth looked up. "I will not bow," she said, but nobody heard her except the court jester – and no one cared what he thought.

"No, no, NO!" said the lady.

"He will be the wealthiest lord
in all the land. Why, even the rats
in his kitchens will eat from dishes
of purest gold!"

"Hmmm," said the tabby cat,
as she licked her paws. "What use
is gold when you are not loved?"

"Exactly so, little one," said
the jester and he shook his head
so that the bells on his hat jingled.
The baby smiled and held out
his arms. "Exactly so."

Years rolled by. Day after day, and month after month, the mighty lord sent armies to crush the kings who lived nearby, and sometimes his soldiers won, but more often they were defeated. The lord grew poorer and poorer, and this did not please his wife. She grew meaner and meaner, until she counted every bite of meat and every sip of water.

And the baby?

He was christened Thorfinn, but his father always forgot, and his mother never remembered. He grew older and taller, until at last he became a young man. He liked to talk to the jester and the small tabby cat, but his father made him pore over ancient books – books about the best way to win battles. His mother made him study spider-webbed spells that promised to show him how to turn pebbles into gold.

On Thorfinn's eighteenth birthday there were no presents, but his parents met to talk about his future.

"It will soon be time for our son to marry," said the lord. "He must marry the daughter of the most powerful king in the world."

"No, no, NO!" said his wife. "He must marry the daughter of the wealthiest king in the world!"

The tabby cat was sitting on
the window sill.

"And what would Thorfinn
like for himself?" she asked, but
there was no one to listen to her.
Thorfinn was in the library, and
the jester was walking on the hills
and listening to the winds.

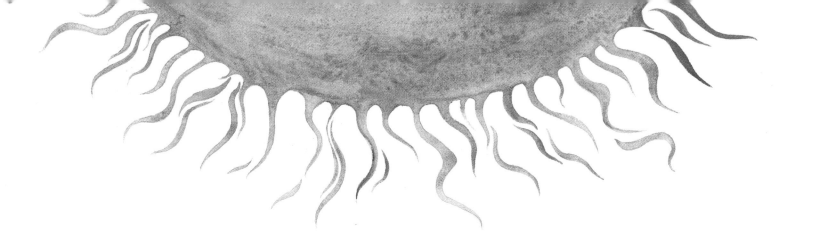

It was the jester who brought the news.

"My lord," he said, "my lady. The King of the Golden Mountains has three daughters who wish to be married. The king is tired and old, and he has divided his kingdoms between them. One will be given all his lands, and power over everything that grows and lives there. One will be given all his wealth, together with his gold mines and his lakes of pearls. The third daughter . . ."

"STOP!" shouted the lord and lady. "We have no need to hear any more! Quick! Quick! Saddle the horses! Where is our son? He must leave at once!"

Thorfinn was standing in the doorway, holding a book. "You are to ride to the Golden Mountains," said his father. "You will go to the king, and tell him that you will marry the princess who brings land and power."

"No, no, NO!" shouted his mother. "You will tell the king that you will marry the princess who brings wealth!"

"No, NO, NO!" The lord banged his fist on the table. "He must marry land and power!"

"NO, NO, NO!" The lady stamped her foot. "Wealth! He must marry wealth!"

Thorfinn said nothing while his father and mother shouted louder and louder. He sat down and stroked the tabby cat.

"I would like to know about the third princess," he said, so softly that only the jester could hear him. The jester smiled.

"The third princess brings nothing and everything," he said. "She brings happiness and love."

"Ah," said the tabby cat. "That is everything."

The lord and lady argued until the sun went down. At last the jester spoke.

"My lord," he said, "my lady. The King of the Golden Mountains has set a task for all those who come hoping for power, or riches, or even merely happiness."

"A task?" croaked the lord. "What kind of task?"

"When Lord Thorfinn comes to the palace," the jester replied, "he will be taken to the king's great hall. The three princesses will be sitting on their thrones. One is pearl pale, with hair as fair as a field of ripened corn at sunrise. One is rose pink, with hair as red as a newly opened chestnut. One is ebony dark, with hair as black as the depths of a midnight river."

"Enough!" shouted the lord. "Which is the princess with lands and power?"

"No, no, NO!" snapped the lady. "Which is the princess with gold?"

The jester shook his head. "Nobody knows. Lord Thorfinn, and all the other princes who come to try their luck, must guess. There will be one chance only and if they guess wrong —" the jester paused – "why, there are hungry wolves on the Golden Mountains."

The lord and lady looked at each other. The jester looked at Thorfinn. Thorfinn stopped stroking the tabby cat and stood up.

"I will go to the Golden Mountains," he said. "I have read and read until my mind is sore, and now I would like to go out into the world."

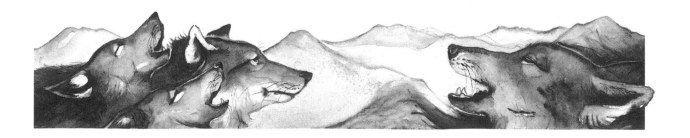

The lord and lady sighed with relief. Even they were unwilling to order their son to risk being torn apart by hungry wolves, but if he chose to go out and seek his fortune? Well, that was a different matter.

His father called for horses, and his mother called for a cloak of golden velvet. The jester spread out his empty hands.

"There are no horses left," he said, "and no cloaks of golden velvet. But the young lord is welcome to ride my donkey, and I have a cloak of wool to keep him warm."

"Will you come with me?" Thorfinn asked, and he bent down to pick up the tabby cat. "You can come too, my friend," he said.

And that was the way it was. The lord and lady were not pleased to see their son ride off to seek his fortune with only a jester and a tabby cat for company.

All they could do was make Thorfinn promise over and over again that he would choose power or wealth.

Long after he was gone, his mother was still calling, "Gold! Gold! GOLD!"

The road to the Golden Mountains was long and hard, but Thorfinn was happy. He stared in wonder as the jester told him stories of the towns and villages and farms that they passed.

"How much you know!" Thorfinn said. "I know nothing at all . . . except that wars cost more than peace, and it is very, very hard to turn pebbles into gold."

The jester laughed, but
the tabby cat nodded.

"Both those things are good
to know," she said. "It is also
good to know that one has
much to learn."

At last the road led up to the palace gates. Beyond was a long line of lords and princes, each hoping to win the hand of one of the princesses. Little by little they moved towards the palace.

From far away came the sound of cries and wailing, but when Thorfinn asked the reason the jester shook his head.

"The wolves will be fat tonight," said the tabby
cat, but she spoke so quietly that Thorfinn could
not hear her.

When Thorfinn and the jester were led at last
into the great hall, Thorfinn's eyes grew wide.
There sat the three princesses on their tall thrones,
and all three were more beautiful than Thorfinn
could ever have imagined . . .

The pearl pale princess
was dressed in a tissue of silver,
and her corn gold hair
fell in shining ripples.

The rose pink princess
was dressed in silks
the colour of an ocean wave,
and her glowing chestnut hair
shimmered in the light.

The princess
who was ebony dark
wore ruby velvet,
and her midnight black hair
curled and danced
around her head.

"It is time for you to make your choice," said
the king. "You may look as long as you wish, but
you may not speak to my daughters. When you
are ready, come and tell me which daughter brings
power, which wealth, and which love. If you choose
correctly then you may choose your bride."

The king's musicians began to play soft music
as Thorfinn stared and stared.

"How can I choose?" he asked the jester. "I know
nothing about princesses, and I have no way of
telling which is which!"

The jester touched his arm. "Ask their father if you may take one hair from each of their heads."

Thorfinn looked up in surprise.

"A hair?" he said.

"Yes," said the jester, and Thorfinn did as he was told – although his hand trembled as he took a hair from each princess in turn.

"That was well done," the jester said. He walked across to the musicians, and bowed to a man playing the violin. The man stopped playing, and the jester took his bow and threaded it with the silver blonde hair. "Now, play!" he said.

The musician began to play, and the tune was harsh and strong. Thorfinn could hear the sound of bugles blowing and heavy armoured feet

marching . . . marching . . . marching.

"Enough!" said the jester, and he threaded the bow with the chestnut hair. This time all Thorfinn could hear was the clink clink clink of coins tumbling and falling, and dulled voices

counting . . . counting . . . counting.

"That will do," said the jester. He snapped off the chestnut hair, and carefully threaded the bow with gleaming black.

"Play," he said. "Play."

As the first few notes sang out,

Thorfinn put out a hand to steady himself.

He could hear the sweetest birdsong,

and children laughing,

and women singing lullabies.

He could hear young men and women

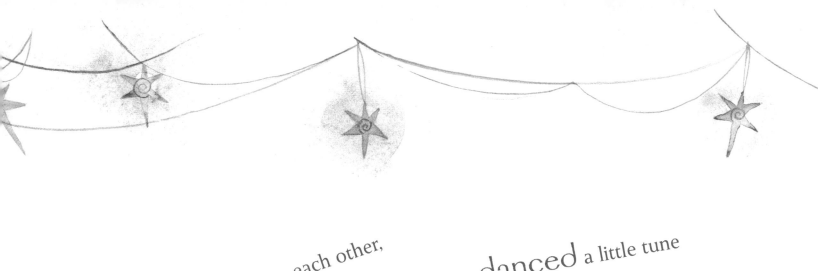

whispering secrets to each other,

and in and out danced a little tune

that was so happy

Thorfinn thought his heart

would break in two.

"Now," said the jester gently, "tell the king what you know."

"The pearl pale princess brings power," Thorfinn said, "and the rose pink princess brings gold. And the princess as dark as midnight brings happiness and love."

"You are right," said the king, and the three princesses stood up, and swept three deep curtsies.

"Choose," said the king. "Choose from Power, Wealth and Love. Choose your bride, and my good wishes go with you."

Thorfinn looked at the Princess of Power, and he thought of his father endlessly fighting wars. He looked at the Princess of Wealth, and he thought of his mother who valued nothing if it was not made of gold. Then he looked at the third princess, and he thought of the long lonely years he had spent growing up in his old, cold castle.

"I have lived with power and wealth," he said, "and they are hard as stone. I have never lived with love, and I do not know what it is like . . . but I think I would like to be happy. I choose the princess who is as dark as midnight."

The king bowed, and the Princess of Love swept another deep curtsey.

"Thank you, my lord," she said, and she smiled a smile that made Thorfinn hold out his arms to her. "Thank you . . .

. . . but I do not choose you."

She turned to the jester. "You are the wise one, and you are the man I will marry," she said. And she took the jester by the hand, and the jester threw off his cap of bells, and the two of them ran out of the king's palace and off and away to live happily ever after.

"Oh," said Thorfinn, and he bent down and picked up the jester's cap.

"Will you not take power, or wealth?" asked the king.

Thorfinn shook his head. "No," he said. "I think I shall travel the world until I am as wise as the jester," and he walked slowly out of the palace, and up the road.

Beside him walked the tabby cat,

and as she went

she looked up at the sun

and she sang.